David Sterne

Marie-Claire Blais
David Sterne

Translated from the French
by David Lobdell

McClelland and Stewart Limited

Copyright © 1973 McClelland and Stewart Limited

This novel was originally published in French
by Les Editions du Jour in 1969.

The Canadian Publishers
McClelland and Stewart Limited
25 Hollinger Road, Toronto

0-7710-1543-7

CONTENTS

ONE

Noon. A siren wails in the town. I am pursued. The town is narrow, its walls are high. I run, I try to disappear, to sink into the shadows of the houses, but everywhere eyes follow me, voices cry, "Thief! Thief!" and I think with a bitter satisfaction, "Yes, that is what I am. But you will not touch me. One does not touch vice." Suddenly, silence. At last, I am alone. Leaning against a wall, I weep and vomit. I weep with disgust and joy, for once again I have eluded them. I am sick, I seem to dissolve on the spot. I am eighteen years old. Tonight, I may die (if not tonight, tomorrow), but that does not frighten me, it is just another source of my grief. I have always lived with sorrow: it has been with me from the beginning, building, growing within me, it will take its final shape now, that is all.

With my handkerchief, I clean my mouth and wipe the sweat from my brow. Oh, how strange is this noon air, so hot and thick, like burning vapors! I breathe and choke, and then I feel better.

I robbed a man in the subway. But what is a man? My small theft cannot touch him. I have set myself the task these days of stealing everything I can lay my hands on. I know, now. And the more frightened I become, the more I know. I do not want you to conclude, therefore, that I am an orphan or that I had an unhappy childhood. One of my brothers is a lawyer;

the other, a priest. Until the age of sixteen, I was a student in the Seminary. Then I renounced the whole thing. My family, my home, everything. I lost nothing. I am going to die, but that is precisely what I have wanted. I have forged my own destiny. What God gives us may not be our own. . . but what I pluck from my miserable entrails is wholly mine!

The source of all this was a philosophical conversation which I had with my friend Rameau at the Seminary. We wanted to be the masters of our fate. Rameau killed himself last October. And here I am.

The subway abounds with self-satisfied men who suffer from the communal malady of possession. It is the sentiment of possession which begins wars. And it is of that sentiment of which I wished to rid myself when I renounced everything. My life, my death, these are my sole possessions. Beneath this threadbare garment, I suffocate, but therein lies my courage. When I steal, it is to cure others of the disease of possession. If I were to kill you, it might well be for the same reason. A self-satisfied man is an insult to me. He asks only to be punished. I am a thief, but it so happens that I am motivated by the sentiments of justice and purity. That will not last, of course. Rameau often spoke of cultivating indifference, even to the point of self-destruction. To me, suicide was never any more than a game. It was simply a matter of escape. Rameau dreamed of a secret level of sublimity; as for me, the decision alone was profound. Little by little, Rameau severed his ties with the world. He withdrew into his own realm, the kingdom of death. Little by little, my suffering filled me. And I began to laugh a great deal. It still happens that I laugh all alone in my room. It seems to me that all the threads of my life snap beneath the rusty blade of my laugh, that no one on this earth is able to amuse himself as I do.

I was running toward the stairway in the subway, the police

were surrounding me... oh, where would we be, my bold partners-in-crime, without the police to watch over us, to protect us, to hug us in their iron breasts, what would become of us without our judges, our accusers... as in the days of my childhood, I have my Odyssey, the murderous crew which pursues me even into my dreams... occasionally, a bullet grazes my skin, oh! my injured knee... that day I was running toward the light of day which was dribbling thinly from the ugly mouth of the subway, wreathed in bloody vapors like the fetid shadows of my dreams, I was running toward freedom, and suddenly I felt the street sinking beneath my feet and the vitriolic sky hanging above my head, two hands gripped me by the shoulders....

My dear mother, I often think of writing to you. You would not appreciate what I have to tell you, your idle ear–oh, I know, no more nor less idle than that of the average woman of your class–would redden perhaps at my account. You were a good mother. There is nothing with which I can reproach you. A faithful wife. My parents are secure people. When they read the newspapers, they do not tremble: their house is solidly rooted in the soil: why should they be alarmed?

Oh, Mother, how I loathe your dull complacent perfection! You have no doubt by now seen my name in the newspapers, or did you not recognize it? You never visited me in the Reform School. Oh, I know, even then I was sliding very quickly downhill: from the Seminary to the Reform School, from the Reform School to prison. Where shall I go now–to hell? or am I there already? My dear mother, your son is no more, if there remain to you any faded images of that lost child of yours, wipe them forever from your mind.

But that day, while nursing my knee, I thought of my mother, and how absurd it was to have run so far, but I could no longer return, and of all those filthy hands that touched me before locking me in my cell, I was terribly thirsty and they refused me drink, the dark dungeon in the Reform School, and the distant sky, blocked from my view for so many days that finally I no longer remembered the words, "Follow us, to the right, to the left!" and the punch in the neck that stunned me, and I felt suddenly a bitter satisfaction rising in my throat, conquered (no, conqueror!), those vulgar blows, that arrest which did no more than test my strength, I wanted suddenly to go even farther, toward a summit of personal glory, toward my own truth, I saw it, it was the green night of my anger, of my cold incurable pride.

I have been swimming for a long time in this feverish sea of my life. From the moment I was placed in my cradle, it was said of me that, my heart being so weak, I could not survive— and look! In the small crystal cage of my being, I used to dream of escape. I was too much pampered and cherished. I became, finally, disgusted with myself. "He is so fragile, don't damage him." Today, I possess great cruel (and ephemeral) strengths that reveal themselves in the guise, not of health, but of rapture, that rapture which is the result of having suffered so much for so long that the whole thing has become, finally, quite ludicrous. How langorously my mother used to lay her hand on my burning brow, running it slowly down my pale cheek. "This child is suffering!" And how he suffered, that child, and how he must suffer right to the end! But that concerns only him. What right had you to pity him? Did he pity himself? And the slow disintegration of the body that everyone tried to ignore. But that was my secret. Was it the right lung that suffered most, or the space between the neck and the shoulder? The pains were never sufficiently pronounced, the anguish never sufficiently profound, I no longer heard myself crying right to the end. Today, I know everything. I was born like a fish. That is what I am, nothing more.

A sickness unknown to the medical world, they say. All I know is that it is fatal.

Each man has a right to say, "I am hell," each man is deserving of unhappiness. And God forsakes him. Forever. For a long while, this single thought pervaded and nourished me. I am proud to be my own creation and nothing more: I walk upright. Even in prison, I did not lower my head. In the hospital, where they drained me of my blood (oh, unhappy day!) and made me spit out my life, I learned to groan without shame (taking care, of course, to do no damage to my teeth). Consequently, I began to laugh a great deal. Like everyone else, I experienced pity, but my pity was directed toward that robust and exalted herd which still kindles my imagination with its gilded, albeit damned, energy: thieves, assassins, all those malefactors for whom the earth is nothing but a dead and odorless garden: they alone, through their vile courage, their baseness, their accursed audacity, awakened in me pity, devotion, perhaps more. For them, with them, I shall drink the cup of torment to its dregs. "God does not understand men," Rameau used to say to me, "but you and I have the capacity to understand ourselves." If I hadn't met Rameau, and if he hadn't appreciated me, who knows, we might have become devout seminarians and not accursed heroes. Heroism interested us only in that sense: to make of it the victim of anarchy.

My name is David Sterne. I have black hair, blue eyes. I am not your typical thief, I do not fit the descriptions of those malefactors whom the police are constantly engaged in seeking. Because I am not wanted, I enter and leave prison with a singular ease. My mouth is severe (with a mean twist to it), my hands are nimble, my smile is wicked–above all, you must suspect my smile. I possess an attractiveness that is slightly hypocritical, though not at all servile. Remove the charming mask from the face and you will see there all the worms which gnaw at me. Michel Rameau used to relate bodily health to a playful intelligence that often fascinated me. "Beware, the lad with the pure heart will do himself in one of these days as he is leaving chapel." And it is done. I alone knew Michel Rameau, the best student in his class. He resembled an angel. He crushed us with his toughness and his innocence. He exhausted his teachers. But I who knew him am aware that he possessed only dark virtues, virtues that led to his destruction. Each of his movements prepared him for suicide: on days of truancy we would accompany each other on stolen motorcycles toward this final course, even the exercise of his muscles seemed to serve his agony, his whole being smiled with disdain. Crossing the swimming pool with the same dauntless energy, he would appear to be swimming toward the low dark shore of his death. But each man chooses his own death. And mine shall be unlike all others, even Rameau's.

Rameau, your mind burned under drugs, while my own delirium grew cold. You lost your appetite. You had visions. I ate like a tiger but my bones remained as spare as your own. "A man must have a reason to exalt his life," you would say. "Whereas I have none, modern man is he who has no reason: he must learn the art of self-destruction before he is annihilated by the bomb."

I didn't listen to you. I meditated, my face pressed against the bars, probing with the tip of my tongue the slivers of ice which I drew into my mouth and melted there, musing with a rank pleasure. . . .

"So, you are not well?"

"Your back? Your belly?"

"Everything, I'm a wreck."

"Don't complain, my friend. You have a teacher, a ferocious mistress. She is misery. She is a custodian from whom you will not escape alive. We know that. Don't torment yourself. Repeat calmly to yourself that you are going to die. That is all."

I didn't listen to you, Rameau. I had seen the doctor that afternoon. I kept repeating to myself that I was lost, and I couldn't suppress a small dry shudder of rage from passing through me. "Remember that we are all condemned to die," Rameau said, "we shall celebrate with champagne, we shall thoroughly enjoy ourselves, count on me. . . ." And, outside, the sky was heavy and grey, above the church, the long drab buildings, the dirty streets, the sky was like a dark grumbling beast, brewing its menace, ready to pounce. . . .

"I'm cold."

"No, you are frightened. But I shall teach you how to overcome that. I shall show you the way. It is simply a matter of mastering death. That is the trick. I can teach you that. It is the only thing which interests me anymore. After all, what is the difference between you, whom decay will embrace tomorrow–or, at best, in six months–and the soldier who will die tonight on the battlefield? Both of you will be annihilated. Wake up, David, have courage, take your death in your hands and look it in the eye, slap it hard in the face. Don't be like the soldier, don't let death take you unawares."

"It is not you who speaks, it is the drug."

"It is the prophet, listen to him."

The violation of things, it was he who taught me that, the

violation, the essence, the knowledge. He stripped away all appearances, he threatened, he destroyed, he trampled on love to render homage to his own desires.

Together, we seduced young girls, then forsook them. Then seduced again, to see whether in the end we might not be able to love those empty shells which drained us. They were no more to us than a frontier which had to be crossed: beyond lay marvels, perverse and profane. We embraced evil all the way to its consummation, and consumed it like stale bread. Prostitution had always been for us this magical roof rotting in the shade, this protective covering under which lay a whole world of seductive debauchery, offering one day with complicity singular joys that, the next, would escape us in dreams. My poor blighted flesh, who down there will despise you for a nocturnal folly? (Women loved me, I recall, without understanding me, for from the moment I sensed death within me, I lost all interest in virgins.)

Julie Brec was the last girl I knew. "I pity you," she said, "and I pity myself, we shall be so unhappy." But already she was addressing herself to my dead conscience. "Go away," I said to her, "I am not interested in love, not even that which I take by force." Do you remember, Michel Rameau, snickering over my shoulder? I see again the black pupils of your eyes peering out of the shadows: "You're hurting me." And Rameau's laugh passing over me like an icy wind. It was autumn. You had taken me into your confidence: I seized your secret and crushed it in my hands like a bird. You were coming out of school, I recall. We went to a concert. Then Rameau suggested a walk in the woods. You were lying like a corpse in the leaves. The odor of mushrooms tightened my throat.

You are wrong, David, so wrong, forgetting the child that you were, sitting in the shadows, those dark shadows which were your protection–your parents caressed you, you drooped–oh!

those long hours sitting under the tree and things working themselves out within you, obscure things, seeing the long day of your life unfolding before you, a life without hope. . . . "David, what are you doing? Tell me the truth." You did not reply. It was the first silence, the first evasion. "I shunned them."

"You have made of yourself a gravely responsible being."

What did my mother see, then, through the veil of her tears, flocks of students babbling under the trees, the white dust at her feet? Did the wicked son even listen to her? Confusedly, perhaps, yes, he recalls having seen his mother weep. It was strange, ironic, to be the son of that woman. It was curious to find himself standing there, insolently leaning against a tree. We were looking at each other, my mother and I. Finally, she said:

"You have changed so much, David."

"We have no choice but to expel him. He is dangerous. I am sorry, Madame, but it is my duty to tell you that. We must let him go."

The solitary flame which consumes me leaves no trace of my soul.

Before my Spiritual Director, my mother promptly prostrated herself:

"The wretched child," she said.

At the Seminary, I often had the sensation of drinking my own damnation like a bitter wine. Rameau and I were both condemned to solitary confinement within our own skins. Less so, alone; but always, together. Solitude is a mystery as impenetrable as gold. Notwithstanding the disorder, it sometimes happened that I would see myself as being perfectly chaste; and chastity of this sort is, of course, not at all appreciated by the world. I dwelt in the cold, bathed in a terrible radiance. How is it, then, that they should want to discover what lies beneath my skin, that they should try to penetrate the dark recesses of my skull? At the Reform School, they knew nothing about me.

At the very moment that I utter these words, my life flies apart, I lie, I continue to lie: I sense the many layers of lies which make up my being, reconstructing, not a credible portrait of myself, but a false and equivocal model which may yet resemble me slightly, who knows? Today, I am a thief; tomorrow, I may be a saint. Today, I save my life; tomorrow, I may lose it. The face which I present to the world ceaselessly alters. If you were to ask me to be pure, I could maliciously feign innocence. I am constantly changing, no one can get hold of me. At the slightest approach, I vanish. Though I drink from all cups, my thirst continues to grow. I admire no one so much as the liar who is capable of lying, the lecher who is capable only of lechery; as for me, I am capable of everything: I spread myself thin, I destroy, in the end I often become my own victim. The models upon which I have shaped myself are too numerous to mention: my face is jealous of my right hand, my left hand of my brow. In me, everything is conflict, ardor, waste. But I walk straight. You see it, under the noon sun, famished, still pursued and persecuted, yes, I walk straight.

Rameau gave birth to his suicide, I to my fall. But I have not become the prince of thieves. I am still irreproachable. My hair is too clean, my teeth too white. "He was one of our most promising students," my Superior used to say, "but God, as we know, denies His light to him who seeks to lose himself."

"A wall of indignity between us, my son!"

Child well nourished by my parents, I did nothing but

16

dream of hunger, though I did not live that dream. Then one day someone said to me: "Hunger, my child, for me, there is the door, open it, follow me," and I followed, while from the porch below there rose to me the sounds of familiar voices inviting me to slumber: "No, do not sleep, loose the filial bonds, you who lie huddled there beneath the scented sheets; rise, go out into the cold night. . . " And I went. I left. Someone whom I did not immediately recognize was calling me.

"Smoke with me, Rameau said, it is my last cigarette. I am going to jump from the chapel belfry tonight after vespers."

I looked at him suspiciously.

"That sort of thing is too childish even to be amusing. But you can always try it if you feel like it. Don't ask me to feel sorry for you, though, I can't do it. I communicate with no one, and anyway what is there to say? You say, "I am suffering, I am going to die." And I repeat to you, "Very well, then, Rameau, suffer and die, and let us say no more about it." "

And now, I am plagued with this same thought: to put an end to it all, slowly, irrevocably: to embrace all vices, then to extinguish myself. . . .

My turn has come, Rameau. Now it is I who suffer and I who will die. And you, I see, cannot abstain from smiling.

Young man whom we have pitied, you are yet a child, you belong to one of our more respectable families. . . like the prodigal son, approach your father, beg his forgiveness, he will take you in his arms and brush away your tears. . . repentance, my child, is an austere virtue, repent, repent. . .

Oh, my father, you who are warm, my father whose goodness so afflicts me, my kind, venerable father, you who enjoy the divine blessings of authority and influence, my inflexible father, too good, too gentle not to be wicked, my father, consider now the one who runs, who trembles under an unfriendly sky, see the poor room which awaits him, the cold bed, the nibbled bread on the bare table. . . and then, as it must be, my father, close your eyes and sigh deeply: "Lord, deliver us from evil. . . "

Don't go back in, David. Your room will be damp tonight. I want to talk to you. I am your friend, your brother. The reflection of your damnation, the dark secret part of yourself, your master, your slave, I am your breath, your inspiration, listen, I want to talk to you. You have seen me in the grey country of your dreams, my face was veiled in mist and my voice came from afar, but you listened to it attentively as if it were a sinister chant. Let me guide you, I shall liberate you from your body and your soul, your blood will flow silently upon the withered grass, remember this invisible bond between us, David, I am not one of those whom you can ever abandon, no, I am he who will always possess; you cannot escape my vigilance, I am the lover of that shape which I have given you, you belong to me.

She says to me, "Come, I will hide you, they won't find you. Oh! I know those sirens, accusing voices, they are familiar to women like myself (Watch out for the step) we won't be alone, there are always people in my place, they're not all as nice as you, follow me, you can't be more than sixteen, fifteen maybe, what a young rascal. I'm going to look after you like a mother, is this the first time you've been here?"

I was on my feet, but they continued to shout at me, "Accused, on your feet! The nature of this theft, gentlemen, is inexplicable."

Oh! torture me, black-robed judges, I will not say a word.

"I wash my hands of your case, I abhor.... That smile! Gentlemen, did you observe that smile? There is a decided perversity here: not only theft, but prostitution; of this unequivocal dissipation we shall not speak; all the anomalies, all the amoralities, are present in the nature of this young man, who, I repeat, gentlemen, is from a good family...."

Go to your father   throw yourself at his feet   say
one word only and we shall accept your excuses
the errors of youth are not eternal   repent
be reasonable
Will you not have pity   your family   your country
One day in the progress of civilization   in the
development of human thought   there will be made
a great discovery which will save humanity
That the long-awaited day should arrive when
extermination camps will be opened for the likes of you
DAVID STERNE Dream of the deliverance of men of
good will
We, the poor victims of your crimes and follies
The father who returns one night from the factory and
chops up his five children with an axe
Will, I assure you, gentlemen, know the same fate as you
    DAVID STERNE   Exterminated
Not shot   painlessly exterminated
Not tortured   we are not cruel
Oh! unnatural beasts who have an appetite only for
    blood blood blood

War alone is noble lawful
But your war is impure damnable
Thieves murderers criminals
To death   To death
And the sadist who disembowels women   little girls
  Exterminated
    Is that not the only solution, gentlemen?
To put an end to the ravages of the David Sternes
of this world?
   "The only solution, I fear, Your Honor."
   David Sterne, you may sit down.

They shot me in the back, in the head, streams of blood gushed from my mouth, my ears, my nose, the pain was nauseating, suspended there in my own filth, I heard the whip whistling against my bones, humiliated, hanged there, I smiled, I heard their gross laughter in the empty spaces beneath my feet, they killed me and killed me and killed me, and when dawn arrived, they said to me, Return home, present yourself to the executioner at eight in the morning, we wish you a good night.

Delivered up to the debauch, I do not experience its pleasures, but only the violence of fleeting painful sensations. My own body remains a stranger to the enjoyments which they procure for me: the flesh of others disgusts me. Enslaved to a man or a woman, I know only cruelty, boredom. The abyss of pleasure will never be for me any more than the inferno of my self-disgust. My love-making is reserved henceforth for corpses.

Base servitudes, I lingered on my way to you

If I ask you as a friend   this indecent bequest
Will you grant it we don't need to go up to my room
No, we shall stay here, we shall not be seen,
oh! what a stench
of foul tobacco
I recall
He pushed me up against the wall   it was night
    night is good
                          don't you agree
I felt his icy hand slipping beneath my coat
He could not see my face   I could not see his
                                    Student?
Yes
    Are you looking for work?
Yes
What a lovely night   listen   there's an ambulance
A rough district   this
Yes
Were you in prison?
                  Yes
How much do you want?
                  A cigarette
                  Do you come here every night?
Three times a week
                  Goodbye.

May I offer you a coffee? My name is François Reine, student
in law. We have a great deal in common, you and I. I, too,
want to reform the social order because I no longer feel a part
of it. You are unhappy, I would like so much to be able to help
you, to imbue you with some ideal, David, why do you not
look at me when I speak to you? I understand, you live as you

21

do because you are poor and misunderstood. A man must earn his living. Misery is so shameless. It is not you whom I judge, David, it is the misery which has driven you into prostitution. What we lack in our lives is a moral code, youth has lost its passion for justice. You understand what I am trying to say, it is just that I cannot bear to see others suffer.

I have been told repeatedly that such an attitude is a weakness. But I cannot believe it. Join me for dinner. You look hungry. I am your friend. I thank God for having brought us together. It may be too late, but that is of little importance. It has been raining all day, your clothes are drenched. Poor boy! Do you have no parents, friends? No? Why don't you say something, I so much wanted to talk to somebody.. . .

David, poor prodigal child, it is I, your Spiritual Director. Though you are lost to us, David, and lost to yourself, I do not cease praying for you. It is I, Father Antime, I bear single-handedly the weight of your defenceless soul. The ripe fruit of your vocation has fallen.. . . Oh! my child, how I pray for you! The white light of noon blinds you, the whole town watches you, all eyes observe you, women pray for you in strange churches, you can no longer escape the justice of God, not today, David Sterne. It is I, your old friend, Father Antime, see how I have aged since last you saw me. I have grown old. Oh! sweet lamb, I see you again on your knees, the victim of anguish, the helpless prey of cunning pieties which suddenly possessed you: "Within, the monks pray while, without, the world burns." You and Rameau, Rameau and you, in the corridors of the Seminary, silent, menacing, that look of contempt which you always had for me, poor priest, staggering old man whose lisping stupidity made you laugh during the Sunday sermons yes I know it I know everything you stood there at my side you and Rameau with this very simple very clear idea of crushing the insect that you took me to be "Propel Father Antime into infinity" you said and it is true that I was near-sighted but it was you who put that ladder there in my path you caused me great pain my old legs are not supple I repeat, David, I do not cease praying for you.

Fearful and restless, Rameau and I were on our knees in the bushes, keeping watch. Rameau told me to go and sleep in the farther shadows. The danger seemed to be diminishing. He was not frightened, he said.

"The first rape, said Rameau. And I am weary, so weary."

"Did you hear something?"

"It is only the wind. No one could have overheard us."

I realized then that he must never have been a child, and that he would never be one. He was like the sterile incarnation of my suffering. I gazed at him with fear. (Several moments later he collapsed against a tree and I could see, beneath his partially-opened shirt, the smooth white skin of his chest. He was fourteen; I, thirteen.)

"To know everything," he said, "is to suffer."

"Let's not try to understand. Later."

Again he said, "You must sleep, it is now two days that we are on the road."

"I cannot sleep, I said, I am frightened of you."

"Why, then, did you follow me?"

I did not reply. I was falling asleep.

"Death alone is ours," Rameau said to me, "and we serve it so badly." His was the essence of an adventure without memory, though I do not expect you to understand that, and I see again his shadow leaping from the belfry, Rameau, victim of suicide, prey of a harsh and bitter heroism: of course, he had read a great deal, that is what you are thinking, isn't it? but surely we have the choice in life whether to be master or slave: if not, what is my existence, what am I but a broken corpse: and his dark blood drying slowly on the cold bare stones of the street

Rameau your crushed body what has become of it tell me
Allelujah Allelujah   and the others praying
Soft silent prayer soothing as a bath
Merciful body of water into which you dip a foot a hand
Then all your weary body   and there you are
swallowed up
In the mud in the salt in the water
Lord have mercy on us
Miserere   and all the litanies lying like a thin froth
on the lips
   "I beseech you, my children, do not leave the chapel
before the end of vespers"
We heard a cry   a faint cry
Father
Keep your seats
Have mercy Lord
And the young man who nonchalantly took the last flight
towards his crucifixion
How strange, Father, that on such a lovely May evening
How strange that a seminarian by the name of
Michel Rameau
First in his class (Oh! that brilliant race
of little faith)
Took that fatal   forbidden   leap

May he rest in peace
                    In peace
And the following day, I went on as usual with my classes.

Oh! my forsaken mother, I often think of your richly-laden
table, the lavish meals you set before me   the burning
coals of my hunger   and then it was winter and my fears
were laid to rest beneath the snow
But today   I am my own nourishment
And I choke on myself
You did wrong, David, the world generously opened to
you
its door
we were at one with each other in the proud bosom of our
family drinking the milk of tradition   of allegiance
yours will be an honorable life like that of your father The
path is laid   follow it
The fraternal clan smiles upon you
In the ancestral fire   you will flourish
Here in his study sits your father   an historian
As was his father   before me and   as you too
will be
At least you can choose a diplomatic career like
your uncle
Or the priesthood like your brother
Oh! David, you have caused us so much sorrow
We who gave you everything
We who were always there   a fountain of advice
of caution   of wisdom
The bonds of blood are so strong between us
Mother and child my dearly-beloved son my poor sick
child whom I cherished loved adored
      I no longer know you no longer know you

You have done wrong.

I reproach myself with nothing, my only home is the country of my freedom, I am engaged in several trades, not all of them honorable, but of what interest can that be to you? I sleep little at night, I go abroad, my impiety directs me, it is true, but how does that hinder your sleep? I am not wise, I enter your houses at night, I await you on the threshhold whenever you return late, sometimes with a knife in my hand, but I am not dangerous, I am your guest, like death I pass by, I touch, I kill.

"Give me something to eat and drink, that is all I ask."

You stand there before me, nervous, distraught. "Call the police." You fill the air about me with noise: I leave as silently as I came.

Of what importance to such model families are the pleasures of my nights, what do you know of the bars which I frequent, the streets which I walk? Wrapped in your golden sleep, huddled in your myth of warmth and serenity, you know no misery like mine. Ah! but for how long? The world is fragile, beware, a single spiteful star in the heavens and you could be slaughtered, extinguished, by the thousands.

But no, within the divine walls of a world constructed in the image of your dreams, what is there to fear? And, indeed, it is not only God who protects you; it is this mighty army of defenses which you have erected about yourselves, this political fortress which prevents death and destruction from taking you by surprise these arches these corridors these walls piled high with miraculous bombs ready to be discharged at a moment's notice (Of course, none of this is more than symbolic, such attacks have not taken place, but one must be prepared for all contingencies, every moment is an occasion of peril, will they attack from the front or the rear? no one knows, that is why we must consider every possibility) oh! sleep, men, under the wings of the metal birds of destruction you have nothing, nothing to fear.

It is I who must lie in wait. And you, lovers, intoxicated with each other, entwined in each other's limbs, I tell you this: tomorrow, you shall be torn asunder.

I did not say that you were responsible for what
happens to me; why, therefore, should I consider myself
responsible for what happens to you, even if it should
happen at my own hand? I have drunk the gall of your
justice–oh! your justice is beautiful, gentlemen,
you may congratulate yourselves. Never have
I gained
so much glory as before your tribunals
David Sterne the thief   David Sterne the Exterminator
(And the young man whom we propel into his cell
on the toe of our boot)
No courtesy for the condemned
Oh! my enemies, how I pity your spite, it alone nourishes
and sustains me.

You cannot deny, said the Judge, that we have been very
patient with you, we have performed our duty, and we
continue to perform it, but you, young man, abuse our
benevolence, you test our endurance, now, make an effort,
that is all we ask, be attentive, rouse yourself from
your revery, a little courage, it is really quite simple.. . .
You are witnesses   this young man is as cold as a stone
His arrogance defies us
He is absent yes it is his absence which confronts us

"What, are you finally awake. . . aren't you ashamed of yourself?"

"Gentlemen, the lash, eight strokes"
My breast split open, my eyes filled with liquid images
If only you know how seductive I find this sudden dream
of torture
At the first blow   no more than a murmuring brook
a tiny white stream   wherein suffering flows
Imperceptible   silent
But as   the punishment   grows and as the bent back
weakens with pain   there issues   suddenly
Oh! a burning sunrise out of the riven flesh
(and the night, as you know, will not come)
And there erupt within you tempests of pride
of delight
An inexhaustible anguish which spills out in hot tears
And there you stand, weeping, smiling, stricken and
                                                    stunned
Under the sudden sharp slap on the face
                    With your torn broken body lying
at your feet
Small battered
            drum.

In a hushed voice, my mother asked, "Father, would you please tell me what my son has done and why you must expel him."

The Superior blushed. His voice was heavy and sad. He spoke of sin, clandestine sin, he allowed his spirit to wallow temporarily in the muddy waters of this swamp, he suggested, he he hinted, but he said nothing. "Oh! Madame, these are things of which one does not speak!

Twins, Pierre and Samuel Martin. Their sly, timid modesty. Twelve years of age. Beguiling as grasshoppers, they desired nothing else. We awaited them in the yard. They knew everything. No questions. One undressed and spread his skinny legs to the sun.
  "How long have you been doing this?"
  "Two years."
  "Do you enjoy it?"
  "Not always."
  "Fear of the superiors?"
  "Some of them prefer that to God."

During one entire month, they returned every night at the same hour: but Rameau was by nature capricious, others replaced them, we became bored so quickly, a great acidic boredom entered my bones, my belly against the ground, I felt the sour boredom inhabit me like hunger, we made love with everyone, everything, fighting nonentity, because it was nothing to us, you see, neither beauty nor ugliness, it was only the emptiness of other adolescents in other deserted rooms, lying awake at night over their caresses, their treasures, primeval shadows plucked beneath the sheets, for Rameau and me the party was over, an entire precocious season during which we were able to love nothing, neither the one which was looked upon as a foolish beast, nor the other which escaped clinging to the neck of that beast, and Rameau saying, "If I weren't so tired, I might be happier," and at night, the tight embrace of those thin and passionless bodies, turning onto my right side,

I saw things moving on the wall, circles, faces, oh! the arrant tumult, the pain, from such a distance now I recall the anguish of dying, and Rameau calmly and obstinately saying: "You should try the drug, it would help you to forget the pain."

My vices and I have always lived in separate entities: there bloomed within me, then, I recall, only the most silent indifference, a naked peace like that of the desert, though it was not the desert.

David Sterne, you have tried everything, we know that, you pass like a fire over the earth, carrying with you the whole genesis of disaster, oh! yes, we know all that, the tribunal is impatient, the society which raised and nourished you asks only the right to abort from its womb this most miserable fruit of the age, the virtue of our daughters, the candour of our sons, the property of our fathers, oh! to all this you are totally indifferent
stand, face me, and listen to what I have to say,
I am the truth, the pith of the truth, the indestructible justice of men
you are lost   David Sterne
I repeat it   you have scorned our forgiveness
like a fruit too green
we can no longer   we can no longer
understanding   forgive   wait
          our pity has run out
     we have done our best
     but you did not understand
     it is enough   enough

"Finally, David Sterne, one last chance. Implore our clemency, and we shall forgive."

"I spit on you, gentlemen."

My friend, François Reine, was walking at my side: I shall
speak to you frankly, David, right to the end I shall
retain the naïeve belief that nothing is as beautiful as
revolt, I admire your discontent, do you believe that I am
capable of saving others?
(He turned upon me a burning look)
You think I am a fool, don't you?
Yes, you are a fool, Reine, I do not even bother to listen
to you
(The wind ruffled his thick curly hair)
It is very kind of you, Reine, but I do not like to hear
people
talk of salvation
(He resembled a sheep)
Awkward, his shoulders large, he moved down the street
I have confidence in you, David, you are a victim of this
terrible
social tyranny
under which we live
Come to my place, I shall give you a Bible
it is all I have
He lived in a poor room with bare white walls
A crucifix on the wall, an iron cot, that was all
Read the Book of Job
                    No
One verse, you will see
                    No
I haven't the time to read the words either of God or of

men
My days are numbered
The words I read have no form, the music I listen to
has no sound
    too bad I used to be a Christian, now I. . .
My political opinions do not interest you, I see
At night I awaken and I think of the hunger
in Latin America
in the Indies   throughout the world
And you   that does not awaken you at night?

                                        No

                            I never sleep

The victims of war
I used to be a Christian but that no longer makes
any sense
It is true that my thoughts are intense   inconsistent
but it is not permitted to a Christian to be
a revolutionary
I have tried very hard in this little room
To wed myself through privation and abstinence to the
suffering of men
One becomes as pure as a column
Then slowly all feeling is lost   everything
becomes abstract
Do you understand what I am trying to say

                                        No

What is there to understand
Chaos   I awaken at night   I think of that
I think also of you
    I am always afraid that they will throw you in prison
                            while I am asleep
    I study but there is no sense in that   exams
there is surely more to life than that   one becomes

abstract yes that is it
   The muscles sleep   the spirit becomes a single
painful sensation
   "Do you want this old Bible?"
   "No, goodbye."

We love but one thing in life, our suffering. I cause suffering,
it is as necessary for me as that I should suffer myself. Rameau
and I had our victims, I do not deny it, but who then is so
innocent that he cannot be punished or tortured? Each one
of us is the odious slave of complicity: he who causes suffering
and he who suffers it participate in the same activity. The goat
slaughtered by the cook on the kitchen doorstep seems also
to view death through our anxious eyes. Therefore, François
Reine, try to understand, see the entire wall of horror which
separates us: solace is not my profession.
Go your own way.
I am indiscreet   yes   but will you tell me
How all this began (a giggle escaped my lips)
For there was certainly a day when you succumbed, David,
To a curious impulse
Yes the sun which one regards with sudden insolence
   Do you remember   David
There was certainly a day when you sensed
This savage force   a beginning of all that
   "A beginning, yes, but not an end."

The loins the back icy with a torrid sweat yes but what
activity I engage in think of that I never cease day
or night
Like a spider or a mole

I play the sentinel   I extenuate my muscles   it is
what I want
Immersed in the work of misery
Not a fissure through which I may escape
A miner without a lamp, but whether or not you forgive
me for that, it is what I want.

I sleep little, though at times sleep takes me by surprise. I
dream a great deal, and my dream is often the same. I am in
a bar, surrounded by festive friends, it is dusk, we are drinking, smoking, existence weighs very lightly on our shoulders:
and, suddenly, I detect about me a strong putrefying odor, I
come back to myself and I notice that Rameau is behind me,
seated on a coffin, smiling at me. I know that this coffin (in
appearance a bench) holds a great number of corpses but
Rameau seems to be unaware of this fact. I try to tell him, to
make him understand with signs, gestures, but he continues
to smile. The dream always ends right there. I cannot bring
myself to sleep more than three hours a night.

On other nights it is the spectre of myself which I see in my
dreams: I am in the final stages of an illness, on the point of
death, what an enigma that this strong spirit should drown,
that the carrion of this body should vanish down a foggy road
. . . . There is also the apparition of an unknown murderer
who seems somehow to be myself, though I do not recognize
myself in it, a young man sitting upright on a hospital bed, as
white as a winter dawn, a bleeding sore in his throat, gazing
out at the world from the depths of enormous pale eyes: this
young man seems to me without grace, sometimes attired in
grotesque hospital garments into which, for some strange

34

reason, his body has been tied. And I hear the voice of Rameau saying, "Are you feeling better today, David?"

But I cannot reply.

It is summer the window is open upon the night
Oh! a night filled with girls   a night bereft of
all purity
It is right that they   should sleep chastely   beneath
their thin cotton shifts
The guardian angel has fastened the door   but has
forgotten the window
The casement of wolves   the department of ladders
It is toward this which I climb
                              And my shoe scraping on the stones
After a night of drunkenness (and that debauchery which
excites my heart)
I leap into the shadow of the bed   a smooth throat
cheeks heavy with sleep
Quiet if you make a sound I shall kill you
So   she   says nothing   resists a little   weeps
     but I am gentle
and console her   come now come now do I look wicked
No no I'm scared oh! Mother
                              she won't come be sensible
Mother
There there I'll be nice   you see   what is your name
Don't cry   I am tired
Yvette
     is it only of her own comfort that she thinks
                              time passes as in a dream
Yes a dream   we float we drift in a nebulous boat
Yes (if Mother knew but she cannot know I am sleeping)

A light breath   on the right breast   what is it?
We are submerged   what happened?
    The young man like a wild furtive animal
    his brow his eyes hidden beneath his dark hair
   "Little courtesan," he says
    And departs.

Rameau, you remember, the miraculous needle, it was a time of escape, but you escaped alone, seeking the peak of the image, as you called it, the prophecy.

    "Stripped at last of all morals, I leave the earth, I go to confront the gods."

    But, as for me, I did not budge from my cage. "I see immortal things, why do you not follow me?" And all those bewitching beauties of which you spoke in such an evasive voice, but for me the delicacy had no taste, whole shipments of drugs could not have appeased me, a needle in the arm to fill my body with revolt, I tried to tell you all that, Rameau, but you were so far away, in that forbidden place where the voice of your friend could no longer reach you.

    Noon
This time you will not escape us David Sterne
What a skillful runner you are but beware it is noon it is
the hour
Frantic   you are encircled with light and then
of course we are
stronger than you as you well know but you love the chase
and so do we
A young police officer who resembles you a little but who
is not you

leaps excitedly onto his motorcycle as if onto a horse
and crosses the town as if it were a small forest filled
with foxes
Ah! we shall get him   it is his first thief
He has tears in his eyes
a little frightened of course
he trembles
But what a firm line to his jaw
It is he who shall carry the game
                              he has vowed it
How beautiful is the face of energy   courage
Father Antime said it well
   "One must not disturb the order of things"
At this moment you might be in the Seminary sitting with
your fellow students reading in the lamplight instead of
running this fearful course   Father Antime
loved you   surely he told you that
   "Let me save your soul"
But you followed only your barbarous instincts
perish then
   "You have gravely offended God," said Father Antime
And he was right
Offend me Lord even as I have offended thee
A policeman a rookie the same age as you   eighteen
years old
Sits high on his motorcycle   smiling with pleasure
That pleases you   you always enjoyed a chase
   "My little fox   soon very soon my pack of hounds will
assail you."
But you are brave.   You run faster.
All these eyes that scrutinize me, these hands that touch
me, I say do not touch me, they glorify my fate, I am
spoken of in novels, I am magnified, I am diminished, do

not touch me, I am a model impostor, do not talk about
me,
I live in a forbidden silence, the eyes of fauns judge me,
what jewel, what delicacy is there like unto my soul,
I am the divine message, listen to me, what foul divinity
is there like unto me, that pleases you, doesn't it,
you cannot resist the temptation to flog me, to cast me
into prison

> I want to know why David Sterne
> that day in the store in full daylight
> you openly committed that tiny theft
> A pair of shoes too big for you

A gesture apart from the world
One must examine it under the microscope   the roots
of things
The divine message, oh yes, that is I   David Sterne

I have come to say goodbye to you   François Reine was
rapping frantically at my window   You cannot come in
Henceforth I hold no more hope of saving you   David
To each his own self-destruction   Do you recall the
journal   *The Idealist's Revolution*
which I founded with several comrades
Come in, then, I said. His cheeks were hollow, he looked
exhausted.
We live in a society of assassins
Stupidity governs the very deeds I dreamed of   It is
nothing if not the triumph of the heart   of love
It is very simple to understand
But the diversity   people do not like diversity

I understand you David   you are governed by the spirit
of asceticism
It is different from my asceticism but that is your affair
I wanted to save you but I was a fool
                              He rolled a cigarette
I smoked slowly   it made me feel better
Is it true that you are very sick he asked me
   "Since my most recent theft they have closed the doors
of the hospital to me."
But I prefer to perish alone.
                              Yes that is more worthy.
A society of assassins David I repeat it
I have written it everywhere on the walls of the subway on
billboards
because it is the truth and the ultimate crime is truth
It can neither be heard nor seen it is the one scandal of
life we cannot survive
Consider that consider all those derisive media through
which pass the truth   the cinema   the television
daily
We are in the presence of a guilty past   of a still
more guilty present
Every day we burn the bread of men   we drop bombs
That to us is the essence of equality
And consider this   it is your future and mine
   "But it is not mine, Reine.   I renounce it."
If only you knew how ashamed I am I awaken at night and
I am ashamed
I think what a hell is this world what an abyss I do not
want to stay here all this spilled blood disturbs me near
or far it amounts to the same thing it is my own blood
the end is near

Stupidity reigns   savage   sad
It may seem like nothing but we shall all be exterminated
in this fashion
There may be a solution   sacrifice
Atonement though I know that you do not believe in that
David
You are made to atone nonetheless you too
As for me I do not suffer it is my misfortune
It is imperative that I immerse myself in suffering
                                        Peace   Peace
It is there that I see it   but we are not useful to men
David   men are machines   I want nothing more to do
with them   goodbye David
    "Smoke another cigarette with me, Reine."
    "No, it is too late."
I do not want to involve myself in this hypocrisy which
                                        governs our times
    "You cannot have life and death, as my friend Rameau
used to say to me. You must choose. Choose, then. And
stop complaining."
Yes it is like the soldier who thinks: either he kills me
or I kill myself   but both choices are criminal
To each his own self-destruction though it is not what
Christ wanted
I cannot believe it
                "And your fiancee?"
                "Oh, you know, love in these times. . . ."
We had a party for workers
                but I lost faith in it in myself in
everything all of a sudden   I lost faith
Goodbye
David Sterne   this is the last time I shall see you
goodbye

Noon. The siren wails in the town. What is a theft? Nothing.
They would kill me for that. For a matter of a few cents, for
a stolen tie. It is because they need victims. I am needed in
this world, I have already said it, each one of us is in some
small way essential, each one of us is not without his virtues.
In the subway people stare at me as if I were in court. On their
faces are written the words, "Not pardoned." They should be
given weapons that they might dispute with each other who
should attack me first. And the children, above all, the insensi-
tive offspring with their protruding teeth, their mean eyes,
their flat empty faces. Whenever I look at them, I am pleased
with my choice of a trade.

My own children will perish in the wombs of their mothers.
The earth will crush them beneath its feet.

The police search   the police search again
And it is I it is I alone   who am too frail to be
frightened and who possess nothing but my suffering
My God what a comedy
                    Why not slacken
                    the pace
the breath
            and let yourself fall into the arms of death?
David it is I your fraternal demon your hell
I am the one the sound of whose voice you so enjoyed
Listen   why not finish it   I am here near you
Collapse   calmly   your agony has lasted so long
My child and not for one moment did I abandon you
Do you recall   an invisible bond between you and me
No no I am escaping
the police are searching

Only your life escapes you henceforth David
I am going to take it to keep it you are mine   I have
said it

My room   my mother   I see myself dead on my bed
but let me run as far as my room
François Reine   Michel Rameau
                                    diverging paths on my route
Here I am whirling in a vortex of memories
I opened the newspaper this morning
                    A young man twenty-one years of age
                                    committed suicide yesterday
                    The young man set fire to his clothing
(I shall not mention the fact that this unfortunate act
took place before the Minister of Nuclear Arms, the reader
disliking this sort of detail) it was with an indescribable
horror that we participated in this scene   before
transforming himself into a human torch the young man
spoke several unintelligible words   the reasons for his
suicide are not known   the victim was identified by
his mother and his fiancee
                    FRANÇOIS REINE student in law
The angels come to gather those who fall during the night
Yesterday François Reine said to me
The hour of pity is agony and pity is patient
He resembled a sheep   he looked at me
over his glasses
                    David the source of my unhappiness
Is that I suffer too little   Goodbye Reine
They struck me on the shoulder on the neck
I no longer know
                    A vivid ball of flame that
spurted

against my bones but did not penetrate me

Do you think that frightens me
I stop for a moment   I breathe   how strange is this
hot air
this thick air of noon   a burning haze

My God My God
Leaning against the wall I weep with disgust
I vomit blood   tears
How can that affect me
The passers-by withdraw
And suddenly it is silent   they begin to forget me
Smiling victoriously the young policeman draws up on his
motorcycle
David Sterne   you have stolen enough   you have run
enough
go back home

The song is ended.

TWO

With a steady pace, Michel Rameau walked toward the Seminary chapel. Slipping on the wet flagstones (Brother Gerard had just washed the chapel with great streams of water, it was a May Friday and cleanliness was the order of the day, indecent cleanliness, thought Michel, in which he could detect the harsh odors of washing-lye and cheap soap mingled with the white perfume of the roses that had been placed at the foot of the altar in honor of the Virgin), opening the door of the sacristy, escaping by way of the darkened stairway to the secret lofty refuge, there where death was his sole companion (Draw near, approach, what do you have to fear of me?). This place of ardor and ecstasy, the belfry, funereal retreat where Michel Rameau spent most of his time dreaming of his own suicide, though sometimes too of God and of suffering, and this word *suffering* turning and twisting within him like a wild animal in a cage. He had read a great deal in the belfry, but recalling now all those books which he had perused, he had to admit that he felt nothing but disdain for them, repeating to himself the very words that he had spoken to David the day before:

"Books are no more than deceits of the imagination and the spirit. Masks to cover the essence of things. I shall give myself up no longer to such comforting illusions."

"Your philosophy," David had absently replied (leaning against the window, he was watching the falling rain), "is to ripen your death. Nothing else."

He had lived a great deal, too. But the final experience aside, what did any life, however scornfully lived, have to offer?

"There are, nonetheless, too many things which I ignore," Michel had said.

Now, David was in the parlour, smoking, smiling, in the company of Julie Brec.

"David, if only I knew why you did that to me."

But he merely shrugged his shoulders. "That is an interesting question, Julie. You came all this way, then, to ask it?"

"I should like to know why you chose me that day," she said, bowing her head.

"Because you are pretty, and because pleasure is ugly. And, besides, it was Rameau's idea. You trusted us. We had to destroy that trust. Is it so terrible, then, no longer to be a virgin?"

But he understood suddenly that she was even younger than he had at first believed, and recalling the scene of the rape, he thought sadly, "The odious thing is that I would do it again, if only to teach myself the meaning of brutality, just as a man decides one day that he must kill himself."

"It is late," he said. "Time to go."

Julie Brec stood up. David shrank from her presence, forcing himself to walk with his head up, though his shoulders sagged like those of an old man. She felt no further anger toward him, a strange weariness, perhaps, but nothing else: if she was beginning to love him, it was without hope.

"Love is the thing which I have the least need of on this

earth," David flattered himself in saying, for he alone knew how love could change none of the folly of his enterprises, none of the terrible agony which was his in an empty room, his throat pierced by a bullet. A poor room which he intended to abandon the next day, leaving, as was his custom, without paying the rent. For he, too, though dying, moribund, already so stricken with that illness which had been caused by the leaden shot in the throat (thanks to the merciful intervention of a policeman in love with duty) and which ate away at his flesh, his life, saving him at last from the atrocious agonies which were reserved for him during those fleeting hours which yet remained to him of his life: for he, too, though fallen, broken (though even yet in the fullness of youth)–he, too, had his habits. Life was still too good to be able to consider death seriously. He had not yet had the time to experience the simplest pleasures which even the proudest of unhappy people allows himself to hope for at that moment at which he knows that all is lost. "I must go away," he thought as he took leave of Julie Brec that day, "I must become intoxicated with all the poisons of my existence, yes, I must go away, I must never return. . . ."

Michel Rameau gave birth to the rare philosophical moments of his life. It was thus in the belfry that he qualified his adventures and set in order his experiences. It had been a long time since Julie Brec had ceased to occupy a place in his thoughts: these young girls dissolved like moths in a flame. One thing alone remained: suffering, and only the suffering could explain and resolve anything whenever Michel Rameau passed before the tribunal of his thoughts. If God were to judge him, he thought, he could not do it more severely than he would judge himself, for having assumed from the outset all the sins "there is not a single crime committed on the face of this earth from which I can excuse myself, neither in the present nor in the future, because I know that my story is the story of a perpetual massacre. That is why I reject the innocence which is imposed upon me. . . ."), having made of himself thus the supreme judge of a past and of a present which he saw only under a painful light, it was of little importance to him to commit the errors which so many others had committed before him.

"How presumptuous!" said David, coldly.

David preferred the rigidity of his own laws. God did not disguise his acts. He would go where he wanted, but alone.

"Suit yourself!"

Occasionally, a moment out of his past would rise in Michel Rameau's mind and occupy the center of his thoughts. It was often no more than a familiar landscape or a particular odour, but a shudder of joy would pass through him as if he had finally discovered something which he had long been seeking. It came from afar. A familiar landscape, a beach covered in snow, an icy sea (strangely silent), a clear birdless sky. He would close his eyes, then, and descend all the way to this level of perfect quietude, moving silently about there for several hours. But suddenly the noise of the sea would surprise him, the snow on the beach would rise up under a sudden wind, and he would be forced to flee: opening his eyes, Michel would understand that he was still under the effect of the drug, and his body would seem to him so light that he thought he ought to be able to unfurl it like a flag from the top of the belfry. The one thing which prevented him from doing so was neither prudence nor fear, but a puerile vanity which he was not at all pleased to discover within himself. His body was no more than a costume, but he could not resign himself to losing it. At the moment at which he abandoned himself to all these images, he retained that aspect of elegance and negligent beauty which annoyed so many of his friends, and although drowsy, distracted, he felt that his greatest fault was complacency, and that consequently he had made only very slight progress in his pursuit of that level of mysticism which was his aim, that too much in the way of appearances, of false bonds (scholarly achievements, perhaps, the hope of vain conquests?) still separated him from the purity of his death. He must wait. The day had not yet arrived. "Sunday, perhaps, after vespers. . . ."

"No, I do not change, I am always the same, if only I could prune away the dead wood of my insolent pride, who knows, the first step might then be taken?"

These scruples amused David. Without reverance for what he called "feminine refinements," he cast upon the confidences of his friend a lightly wicked reproach.

"You ought to plunge into the cold waters of my conscience, that would do you good. There is too much torment within your make-up, too much delirium. I pity you."

"To each his silence, to each his horror," thought Michel Rameau, huddled in the shadow of the belfry. "David will have reason enough to lose himself, I have no advice to offer him." In solitude, Michel recovered his severity, immersed in the muddy destitution of his moral landscape, and at the same time, a violent desire to terminate his association with David, the last barrier between himself and his death.

But descending from the belfry, once again finding David immersed in his dreams, he would think, "It is strange, he was not corrupted in the beginning, it is as if he had invented all of his corruptions, that is why one becomes so stupidly attached to him, I suppose, but is he then redeemable?" Finding David there, it was almost like rediscovering himself, falling into a familiar dialogue, living and dying under the same roof, as if, since David had embraced agony, and himself, death, all was naught, even the friendship which united them.

"To suffer without recompense," said David, and Michel added, "There is nothing, in the final analysis, which can make the soul breathe, even for a single instant. . . ."

Michel respected the difference between them. He allowed David to escape from him, preserving nothing for himself but his own solitude, wherein he considered nothing but his own existence in the world: as for David, to see him suddenly was to understand that, in sickness, he had found the answer to everything and that he was appeased, satisfied.

But it was not only of the shell of his body which Michel Rameau wished to divest himself, but of all traces of servitude capable of aging within him. A man always had too many hopes, even when he believed himself to be rid of all hope. At the very moment that Michel Rameau dreamed of self-liberation, he could still feel the oppression of the life which held him to the earth and prevented him from opening his arms to space. "If only you had been like the others," Father Antime had so often said to him, "you would not be where you are now, my child. What you seek in this quick death is the expiation which Christ offered you and which you refuse . . . ."

"Yes, to be sincere, to live like everyone else, without spite, without regret. . . ."

It is true that it would have been more agreeable to marry Julie Brec than to so brutally seduce her, to inculcate virtue in children than to deprive them of it, to elevate the senses than to debase them. Oh! this sly regret of noble and innocent desires, it would have been so easy to make a success of his life, to have matured gently, but God, who did not love Michel Rameau, had filled him with a violent hatred of the perishable joys of the earth, and for that Michel Rameau rejoiced, as if he had been a warrior picked for a bloody battle. Every day of his life, he was delivered up to this combat, and if he choked at times upon the putrid odours of death and decay which lay all about him, the sudden wind of his impending freedom would always revive him, like that icy landscape, that snowy beach, which appeared to him in dreams and to which it was so good to abandon himself as he might to the warmth of a bed.

"But, my child, your career, your future, do you consent then to forsake all that?"

"What other answer can you give me, Father Antime, you who have scorned me since the day I dared to speak to you of the troubled saintliness of Spinoza? You say to me, 'Everything is contained in the word *substance*, let us talk no more about it. . . .' Give me a legitimate affirmation and I shall believe in your moral precepts! But I amuse you, oh yes, I delight you, how can you possibly take me seriously?

Rameau accused, though gently, dreaming of the next trap which he was about to set, preserving his pride for more subtle revenges, leaving to David for the moment the leisure of displaying his intelligence, his heart, in aggressive arguments which Father Antime seemed to encourage. . . .

"How can a child of your age rebel against true learning? How can you presume to destroy all certitude? Oh, that Grace may come upon you and relieve you of all this vile seeking. . . ."

Litany of lies, extravagant submissions to which David was of the world ("My guilt is historical," he often said to David, compelled to listen, one hand on his hip, his head inclined slightly to one side, saying to himself, "Oh god, I think I am going to vomit," but drunk with dignity in the eyes of Michel Rameau (except in that debauchery which opened to them the door leading to communal labors under a sun so hot that one was no longer permitted to see), he controlled himself, listening with a feigned attention, until finally he was compelled to say in a strangled voice, "Excuse me, Father Antime, I must leave, I am not feeling well."

As for Michel, he subdued his strength in silence. "I pity God," he thought, "who knows how to create only evil. Our single act of obedience, of true faith, was to have consented to be baptized in suffering, and how we are punished now for that...." It was necessary finally to arrest this flood of thoughts, to forego condemning God in front of the others. Father Antime would have had good reason to exclaim, "Ah! how blind is youth, how utterly intoxicated with itself!"

"There is no true virtue," thought Michel Rameau, "no sanctity which does not observe its own reflection in the glass: what a monstrous act of forgetfulness, of selfishness, it is to be happy.... One draws his happiness out of the entrails of others, renewing each time the massacre of the Jews, the devastation of Hiroshima...."

"But no, it is much simpler than that," said David, "one succumbs to a natural temptation, that is all! It is not a crime to be happy! The world belongs to me, to all of us! Each man seizes his booty!"

"No, there cannot be any true virtue," thought Michel Rameau, an odor of mustiness emanating from the belfry and settling about him. "To love virtue for itself is still to remain the slave of one's vanity. Under the rarest and most dignified of ideals, one does nothing but serve oneself, it is always the constellation of self which shines the brightest...."

It was not the same for François Reine who, at that time, was discovering that the only true hero was he who obeyed "the impulse to courage, to justice, the only symbols which ought to govern youth," as he declared during his weekly conferences with militant workers. "Charity is the sole glory. . . ." He spoke well, moved by the boldness of his own words, saying to himself that this was not after all so difficult, and that he was moving each day a little farther in the direction of his chosen goal. François had not seen David since their last encounter. His life at this time had no shadow. He sowed conferences in his wake, brought together students and teachers, and in all honesty and trust, one foot in the faculty of law where he had begun his studies, and the other in the brothels where he retrieved the sheep lost to the fold, what ambitions did not nourish him?

His hands in the pockets of his ragged coat, his nose in the air, sniffing not only the odours of hunger that pervaded his route, but also dreaming vaguely (very vaguely, to be sure) of the delicious meals, served with wine and coffee, which were set before him at his parents' place in the evenings: how was it possible to be so happy? François Reine was part of that much envied group of which it was said, with a slight shudder in the voice, "He does nothing but good. I know of no fault in him." And the day was yet far off when François would, in effect, thank God for having sent David his way, for having thus punctured the festering abcess of his pride: who knows, perhaps by tomorrow, when the time would come for him to consent to the sacrifice of his life, he would have learned a total humility? But, for the moment, François Reine was floating in the sluggish whirlpool of lies, and his joy was profound. (It was here that the drunken child was entertained, that perversion was succoured: what a mysterious comfort no longer to be in the country of barren fig-trees!) But if François walked with hesitant steps toward his truth, Michel Rameau already possessed his, that nocturnal sun the first rays of which were beginning to bathe his icy face.

"My own virtue is the boundless violence of my justice, of my condemnation to death. You are witness, Lord, that my frail death does not know your pity. . . ." But cool, calm, indifferent, the divine quietude assailed the blasphemies of Michel Rameau. How could it be otherwise? Michel wrapped himself in his death as in a betrayed love, he suffered all its secret tortures, all its regrets. And how many young people did not dream, as he did, of embracing the same tragedy, of closing their eyes under the same fountain of blood and light, while this jealous death which was the birthright of everyone and of no one did not deign even to smile upon them? At the same hour, on the same Sunday, after vespers, who knows how many desperate children, moved by the same drunken and deadly thought, were not planning to yield to the same temptation, to leap across that gentle gulf, their lives already spent, and to take their leave at last. . . ?

But Michel was alone. David could no longer come to his aid. The labor of redemption which occasionally lifts souls and permits them forgiveness of one another, was stripped, in their case, of its fruit.

This word *alone alone alone* was suddenly the key to the mystery of the life of Michel
Nonentity alone   Michel Rameau alone   you are going to die
And all about you the void is so clear that if you were to awaken suddenly
Your horror would take you by the hand   prairie of death you see it

These two words forever   dead   alone   he died
alone
My God   how you suffer   but it is not enough
it is never enough
(But he can hear the voice of the Superior saying:
   "I beseech you, my children, to keep your seats. . . .")
And death, when you imagine it, is something else
it is a patient dream   a prayer
Not that rime which will soon seal your lips
Those black roots which will choke your loins
("A strange thought passed through his mind as if he had
called down upon himself some punishment. . . "
But, very simply, David had said, "Michel, you must
come down. . . .")
Everywhere there was this desert this silence this empty
pit which sucked you in
    Come come it is I unacknowledged unsatisfied love
A single gesture and the sun is yours a bed of stones upon
which to lay your head
    "You saw, didn't you, how silently, without the least
disturbance of the leaves, his body fell. . . ."

With measured steps, Michel's comrades were walking
back and forth in the Seminary yard below him.
    "What dizziness,
if one stoops," thought Michel, "all is naught, one has the
impression of breathing the fetid air of a swamp. . . ."
One grey day, much like this, Julie Brec had huddled
beneath her coat, weeping. . . . Oh! what a strange feeling
is this awakening lust from which all pleasure is absent!
Night follows vespers dawn follows night and I am still
dead
When dawn passes over me no one will remember

Everything devours me silently
I see my dark silhouette withdrawing into the night
   "Sunday, after vespers, I shall kill myself."
   "It is a thought like any other."
David smiled, a book of Kant lying open upon his knees.
   "I want to unfurl my body in the wind like a flag,
without a gesture of pity. . . ."
   "That is surely your business."
David smiled, dreaming of the small dry death which
awaited him the following day in a hotel room.
   "Have courage," he said to Michel Rameau, "you know
very well that I shall follow you."
For the first time, Michel Rameau had no answer for
David's contempt.

Assisting at vespers awakened in Michel Rameau bitter
jealousies which he savoured in silence. While praying, one
rendered homage to the absurdity of existence. One said,
"Lord, remove the bread from the mouths of men. Lord, we
adore thy strength which breaks us, thy tenderness which kills
us." God was the father, the chief oppressor, under his aveng-
ing hand men perished, one lived in his shadow as in the
shadow of bombs. In this reign of terror, accomplice of the
folly not only of men, but also of the God who had created
them, how could he, Michel Rameau, permit himself to live?
One must protest, break the bonds with that nature which was
called sovereign, but which was no more than the garment of
destruction. And as for salvation, what was it in the face of the
murder of Jewish children but a dream of the white shore of
redemption? It was too late to expect forgiveness. All men
were in hell. There was nothing more to hope for: one must
kill or be killed.

God of kindness
God of goodness
Pray for us

Oh, how beautiful was that generation of seminarians who prayed! God of pity, God of compassion! From their warm chapel, from their dark dormitories, what did they know of grief? Faces, bodies, whirlpool of faces and bodies, of soft smiles, of dissembled passions, is that what was called living? Michel Rameau, trembling with horror in his belfry, had seen the world as a battlefield, he had walked amongst the corpses of children, the bloody earth had opened beneath his feet. He had seen so many things that he could no longer live: lately, he had not been able to look at David without observing that his friend was decaying before his very eyes. The universe was filled with a torrid stench, it was necessary to leave! "But no," thought David, on his knees at Michel's side, "everything is fine, I have perhaps a year to live, I shall not waste an hour of it, not an instant. . . . I shall try everything, risk all my dreams, a long year in which to do nothing but that, making a monstrous experience of the time which must pass."

David was suffering a great deal, it is true, but even a body wasted by a lingering illness does not tire of its final pleasures, which, drawing one a little each day toward death, are not devoid of an almost visionary perversion, dreadful savors unknown to the man of good health to whom they are a threat neither to time nor life.

"I shall be free, like a thief I shall seize my life, saint, martyr or corruptor, what do I have to lose?"

David passed a hand over his perspiring forehead "No,

no, it is not necessary to fall, don't fall, David, it is too soon. . . ."

Allelujah   Allelujah   I must flee, Michel repeated
to himself
God give me the courage   solitary act
which concerns   no one
but it is my secret revolt silent revolt
    not a sound My hatred of the world crowned in blood
but I shall be
able at last to join
so many others   the condemned man whose execution
will be carried out at dawn
                              in winter
The monks pray   the entire world prays   we love
prayer
It is comforting   it prevents us from hearing the
bitter groan
        of the hanged man
at the end of his rope   You know the law justice
permits it
One must above all protect oneself from criminals
Otherwise they would overrun the streets
This time it is I who shall be executed   curious fate
How does one accustom oneself to it?
Pray for pray for us
Save us Lord who perish
    "Goodbye," muttered Michel Rameau between his teeth.
But David did not reply. No shudder passed over his
face. Michel hesitated yet another few moments, his heart
troubled within him. Still, David did not reply. Then
Michel Rameau arose and moved towards the door.

58

It was cold in the belfry. Tears ran down the face of michel Rameau. He had almost anticipated this final mercy.

"What a contemptible farce," he thought, "I had the weakness to dress myself as if for a funeral, purple tie, black vest, over a clean white shirt, and worse than that, I drank in secret in my room! It is absurd, is that any way to mount the scaffold? Right to the end, I shall be shocked even of the nothingness from which I have emerged." He was so cold that it seemed to him that at any moment his heart must stop beating. "Julie Brec," he thought, "and all the rest of you whom I deliberately abused, and who deserved nothing better, small vicious comrades, adolescents, leprous youths ruined in the seminaries, in the convents, Father Antime, you whom I failed to knock off your tower of vanity and pride, all of you, my friends, come now and help me if you love me so much! And you, my faults, my sins, make haste, if you do not support me, who then will do it?"

Julie Julie you do not remember then? And you Pierre and
Samuel Martin
       subdued   subdued
Little girls   ungrateful women whom the lude smile
followed everywhere in the street
I lived in the world as if in a bed of lust
               no   no
             said Julie Brec
but all the others said yes   and again yes
I was cold   you cannot understand   no fire in these
             icy limbs
   "But it is absurd, again today I see this snowy landscape,
this cloudless sky, these birds flying lightly over this
deserted beach,
down there, perhaps in my dream, was I happy?"

He closed his eyes. The street, so faraway yet so near, at a distance that necessitated his stooping to see it, turned slowly beneath him. "My God, My God," he thought, then his thoughts were interrupted, and he felt his body fall, *irreparable, irreparable,* these words crossing his broken mind, and at once a great peace invaded him, and lying there on the ground, he was afraid to move lest he lose it.

THREE

Farewell, Michel
Rameau. For you, it was the end; for me, only the dawn.
Two days after the funeral, I left the seminary,
and today here I am, in a musty hotel room, losing
my blood! The faun in police uniform has long pursued
me,
has long lain in wait. Now, I am alone. My room is a tomb.
Outside, life goes on. The children play. The sun casts
its pale rays on the leafless trees. Yesterday, a young man
by the name of François Reine burned like a torch before
the eyes of the Minister of Nuclear Arms. Today, life goes
on
I would like to save you (in this street where I put
myself out to pasture, François Reine invited me to
partake in his happiness, in his naieve virtue)
Leave me alone
(I dreamed of pursuing him with indecent gestures)
I do not need you François Reine
                    He withdrew, his hands thrust in his pockets.
  "I shall return tomorrow."
I have thought a great deal, David, I have thought a great
deal about you,
you are right, before meeting you I lived in a dream

(I was not listening to him   I began to walk faster)
the problem of lost souls is insoluble
You are nothing but a dreamer!
I was moving towards poverty with the soul of a rich man
I measured my gifts   I spoke with arrogance
I possessed everything   did I think of God and the world
all that because I had read Hegel   Marx
How to inspire the humble with a pride which they do not
often have even the desire to know

   "I must leave. I have to earn my bread."

   "Where are you going?"

   "To find my next meal, I just told you."

Little by little, out of boredom, I fell into the habit of stealing with neither art nor prudence. The singular pleasure which I had known at the beginning, to use my nose like an animal to smell out a piece of meat or bread, was leaving me now that hunger itself was beginning to disappear. Was it because of fatigue or indifference that for entire days I would not wash myself or trim my hair, then suddenly slip anew into the unattractive costume of cleanliness? In the streets I would parade my bitter and spiteful elegance. Before the laden table which François Reine set before me, I would neither eat nor drink.

   "The proof that you are neither a hero nor a saint is that you are still too much in love with your appetites, those innocent appetites of yours, to live, to eat, to sleep, you are not yet indifferent to habits!"

I have reflected a great deal David   you have reached

a dangerous frontier
You refuse divine grace   an admirable gesture perhaps
Where do you find the strength to live thus deprived
of light
Before you I have learned reverence   impotence
Why do you continue to scandalize me   why do you
confound happiness   joy
But do you know that I am still too happy   the autumn
mornings are so lovely   the dawn intoxicates me
Do you know that I sing while dressing   while walking
to church   I love everything   I love perhaps too
much
   "You do not have the gift of unhappiness, that is all.
How can you possibly understand me?
   "Won't you remain with me a moment longer?"
   "No, I have better things to do than to listen to you."
   "Drinking?"
   "No, making love. Don't blush. These things happen."
   "But human tenderness. . . ."

Farewell, Reine.

   Passions wearied me. As soon as the gesture was consummated, I would turn toward the wall and smoke, smoke endlessly, if only to fill those atrocious lustful hours of dawn. Michel Rameau never knew satisfaction. He did not have the time. As for me, I drank the entire horror of my life, the entire ecstasy, too. Whenever any act is consummated, one breathes at last, one trembles a little, that is all.

I thought of you standing there in that cold street
I saw those nocturnal passersby who whispered in your ear

Indecent words which you heard with indifference
Your indifferent gestures too
Did it happen that you pitied those caresses
What an immense lost joy
That immense tenderness   killed   buried
But gestures are no more than appearances
Who knows your distress   your silent compassion
Your sadness when the anxiety of the senses is asleep
Who knows if it is not pity which you everywhere seek
What then are you seeking David?
     "Dizziness, nausea, incurable headaches."
What is confided to you then by those unhappy souls in
the intimacy of pleasure
so many secrets I am unaware of   this harvest of
confessions which you have reaped David
There is but one secret and that is suffering I used not
to know it
I scoured the flowering countryside on bicycle
I love trees, water, things which for you are nothing but
pleasant images

"Everything resembles everything else, François Reine.
There is nothing so new as to surprise me!
You cannot understand me
my language is a language of violence and blood
crime redeems the criminal   and him alone
There is a wall between you and me
     "Is that wall truly insurmountable, tell me?"
     "Since you love the cross so much, clasp it silently in
your hands, and for once in your life go straight to the
bottom of yourself! It is thus that you shall surmount
the wall!"

An idea came to me but I cannot communicate it to you
A gesture that you will perhaps understand
Care and respect are the virtues which I lack.

"You irritate me," I said to François Reine, in the hope of never seeing him again. But no betrayal seemed to be strong enough to provoke his withdrawal. With what sense of deliverance would I return to my nocturnal friends, those strangers encountered in the streets or in bars, I reserved my friendship for such assassin-silhouettes, men threatened like myself, escaping from their smoke-filled hovels to wander at the bottom of the night, night, that invisible healer wherein circulate, in the alcohol and the smoke, these silent sharks which we are. At dawn, I occasionally found myself in prison, my own solitude disgusted me, I returned home, dragging myself through the streets, alone, always alone.

They steal your watch. They leave you nothing but scars on your cheek. You think, "But did I fight again?" You begin to bleed at the nose, and then you understand.

David   it is I
                    He was rapping on my window
I am cold   May I come in?
There is no fire here
The room is cold   bare
    "But what do you have that is so inexplicably different
you too read Kant and Spinoza
why do we not speak the same language?"
    "You are saying nothing to me, David.
You are mocking me."
The sea of suffering unrolls to infinity
and you are not the Savior's raft   Reine

I do not want your tolerance
society will exterminate me quickly enough. . . .

"I shall prove to you that you are wrong, David."

"Yes, I shall make him understand me, one day,"
thought François Reine, moving down the street.

> *The hills are volleys of mirth*
> *the plains are covered with flocks. . . .*

Oh! this bold joy which permeates all anguish! Would David,
then, never know it? Sitting alone on the bus, warm thoughts
gently invaded him. "David must be saved, his soul must be
taken by surprise." Finally, François returned home, lighted
the lamp, removed his boots, and stretched himself out on the
thin blanket of his bed. Several moments later, he was asleep.

"It's François Reine," said a woman's voice. "Must we let him
in?"

François was knocking again on the door. What was he
doing here on the fifth floor of this over-crowded house?

"I have been sent by the workers' committee."

The woman opened the door. She was a young woman but
she bore the marks of multiple miseries and illnesses. François Reine could see a dozen children behind her, playing in
a room as small as a cage.

"You must excuse us, there are rats everywhere, said the
father, tossing the bread onto the table. We have to give them
our bread, our milk, otherwise they would eat us!"

"There is no chair for you, Mr. Reine," said the mother.

"The rats eat everything we have."

"I am going to be sick," thought François. "I am going to offend these poor people, I am going to vomit before their very eyes."

"You came for the arithmetic lesson?" asked the mother.

Then she disappeared into a farther corner of the room, and returned, bringing with her two pale, nervous children which she held by the ears.

"Here they are," she said, pushing the children brusquely before him.

"We shall begin with the alphabet," said François, feeling strangely that he had in some way offended this family. "I mean to say, reading is an excellent discipline. . . ."

The woman shrugged her shoulders. "We had a table," she said, "but the rats ate it."

One of the boys opened an ink-stained book on his knees. "I. . . I. . . ." he began to read.

The other boy laughed. "I am going to laugh, too," thought François. "Oh! I know I am going to laugh like a fool. . . ."

"I. . . I. . . ."

The child brought the book up close to his face. Bending over the big black letters, he repeated "I. . . I. . . ," but saw nothing.

"How strange!" said the other. "He is blind!"

And he laughed even louder.

"What a hoax!"

"Oh! what a hoax!" said François, and this time he could not prevent himself from laughing with the child.

"My God, what have I done?" thought François. "All these hours lost in sleep!" For three days he had thought only of

David. He had forgotten the list of families he was supposed to visit. Here he was, troubled, tormented, following David on his infernal path, and he was forsaking everything else.

"Mrs. Gobin. . . it is I, François Reine, I have come for the little one."

With a mournful air, the woman opened the door.

"He says he's sick. He don't want to get up."

Then, turning a heavy profile in the direction of the shadows where her husband was scrupulously cleaning his ears with matches, she added, "Ain't it the truth that kid's good for nothin'?"

"Out of work," said the father, "and that good-for-nothin' won't lift a hand to help me."

With patience (for was there not an infinite time stretching before this man?) and a certain absence of mind, that bitter absence of mind which always prompts such unhappy gestures, the man was working deeper and deeper into the cavity of his ear, shaking his head periodically from side to side, groaning about how difficult their life was!

"But the little one?" asked François.

"Who knows?" said the father. "Sleepin', I guess."

Rosalie Gobin appeared suddenly, a frail flower in a black pinafore. François took her into his arms.

"And have you done your homework?"

François and the little girl moved toward the stairway. Glancing into an adjoining room, he was drawn to a sudden halt by the spectacle of Pierre Gobin lying on his bed, twisted in agony, his burning gaze moving restlessly over the ceiling.

"An animal bit him on the knee," said Rosalie gleefully.

A rat had bitten him   the child was right
Yes David on that day   beside that child I understood
that God permits suffering
The ambulance took us to the hospital
the little one did not cry   he was not in pain he said
but as for me I recall that I was sick with disgust

Drinking a beer or smoking cigarettes that stuck to his lips,
David would observe François, entertaining with suspicion
those words which, the following day, he would agonizingly
recall in the empty solitude of his room, not faint and remote
as he now heard them in the coldness of his heart, but close
and poignant, recalling his deliberate rejection of all that
François had tried to say to him.
   "Drink, then, that will do you good."
   "No thank you, David, I am not thirsty."

This ardent melancholy   how could I explain to myself
this disease of listening to François Reine when I was
already moving toward the grave why didn't he leave me
alone
my feet treading the black earth I wanted nothing more
than to descend to disappear to vanish I asked nothing but
that but no he wanted to prevent me from crossing that
threshhold he showed me the crepuscular sun which
flattened itself out on the mountaintop on the farther
side drowsy lakes sleepy meadows scenes of enchantment
bliss
   and my obsession with suffering was little by
   little extinguished
why didn't he leave me alone

"Goodbye, David, I have scarcely known you."

Goodbye Michel Rameau, Goodbye François Reine, each one of us withdraws along a pale road under the moon. Occasionally, I still call, "Michel, is it you?" The night is silent. But, suddenly, Rameau jumps from behind a hedge and signals to me to follow him. We find Julie Brec asleep beneath the trees. Rameau tells me not to awaken her. On our knees in the bushes, we speak in hushed voices. We are dazzled by new possibilities rising transparently in our minds, a delightful harmony governing our thoughts and our actions. "And to think that Father Antime is unaware of such beauty!" says Rameau, smiling. He bends gently over Julie Brec, caressing her eyes, her forehead. Once again he says "Since we are in love with her, we must not awaken her."

On other days, I attend Michel Rameau on the edge of this same dappled forest, but my comrade does not come. Or if he decides suddenly to appear, it is to hit me with sticks or the butt of his rifle. But is it really Michel Rameau? No, only a mirage, an icy shadow. The young man withdraws. From afar, his silhouette once again resembles that of Michel Rameau. I hear the painful sound of his laughter. It seems to be that I am watching the disappearance of a familiar head beneath the branches.

But as for you, François Reine, you continue upon your zealous route more alone than ever: why did I not keep you near me, far from the troublesome society of do-gooders? Unhappy martyrs, loved neither by God nor men! Heaven or hell, whether the flame rises straight and pure toward the dark sky or whether it crackles madly on the dry plain, what difference does that make to us, François Reine, will not the blazing fires of our bodies be extinguished in the same manner? In the hour of agony, do we not rediscover in ourselves always the same nonentities, the same wanting creatures?

To sleep. An hour perhaps. Then to return to the fight. The bed is warm. I feel as if I were swooning with pain upon the breast of a brother. But there is no one here. I listen to the muffled beating of my heart. What passing being, creature or spirit, would not stop to cast upon me some fugitive pity which I do not need?

David it is I   I have come to say goodbye

This time, a gust of wind opens wide the window. Standing in the street, François Reine smiles in at me. "Come," he says, "I have something important to tell you." It is night. An icy wind causes me to shudder. I discover suddenly that I have not taken the time to dress. "We must find some wood and make a fire," says François Reine. But how, on this winter night, infinitely deserted? I would like to flee, to escape my meagreness, to leap out of my naked skeleton, my bones provide me with so little protection. But stopping suddenly, Reine offers me a cigarette and we smoke silently in the snow. Cigarettes burn so quickly that I scarcely notice the flame that runs up the clothing of François Reine and into his hair.

I want to cry out but no sound escapes my lips.

"Warm yourself," says François Reine, "you will have a chill tomorrow."

It is too late. I forgot to lock the door. The policeman has detected my odour. I hear him singing as he mounts the stairs:

Steel jawbone   iron fist

I come as a friend
Let me in
As a friend   to crush your loins
To break your neck   what a good life
    this is
Courage   I am coming my friend
A hail of bullets in the belly
La la la what a good life

"Everyone says I have a good voice," says the policeman, appearing on the threshhold. "What, you weren't expecting me? Not at such a late hour?"

He is a handsome young man, wearing a blue cap and shiny black boots. When he looks at me with his magnificent eyes, it seems to me that God has entered my room. Fear of his anger paralyzes me.

"On your feet!" he shouts.

On your feet On your feet

Two policemen with identical smiles stand on either side of my bed. "On your feet! On your feet!" they shout. "Follow us!"

"He is covered with blood," says one, "you felled him like a rat. There is nothing more for us to do here."

But the other rebukes him. "He might follow us, he is still alive!"

On your feet On your feet
The kinder of the two was the first
to brandish his fist

I'm getting up Gentlemen   here I am

"He is dying," says the one.
"Who cares?" says the other. "Hit him!"
"What exactly did he do?"
"Hit him, hit him!"

My ribs crushed, my arms and shoulders
      broken
But no pain in my sleeping muscles
I fall   they lift me up they beat me
      I fall again   they laugh
They withdraw   the job is done

Out! says the landlady. He hasn't paid his rent for
three months Get out David Sterne And suddenly
I find myself alone in the stinking courtyard of the hotel.
The wind dries the blood on my face. I feel safe here,
among the trashcans and the garbage. In summer, who
knows, I might become a feast for flies? But it is winter,
I am lucky, I shall die slowly. . . .

FOUR

David Sterne is dead. May God have mercy on his soul, *requiem aeternam dona ei, Domine!* As I was saying yesterday to my devoted friend, Abbot Jaloux, it is our duty to pray for these lost souls, *requiescant in pace!*

Oh! what a wicked trick   Michel Rameau
   David Sterne
To make me fall over a ladder   me?
I still hear them laughing behind my back
"Hey, Father Antime, hey. . . "
It is my turn to laugh now
How wise they are lying beneath the earth
Worms beneath them   worms above them

My life was so good in the Monastery of V. . . . A silent atmosphere, immersed in the spirit of God, with its stand of pines, its quiet lake which lay beneath my window, what an ideal place for meditation!

"He has suffered too many calamities, out good Father Antime has lost his reason. But after the night storm follows the dawn."

(The food was excellent, with what devotion did they attend to me in my old age, in all humility, Lord, I deserved that)

Come my children   atone atone
The flowers are blooming the birds are singing

They will receive each day my generous prayers. "They were the prey of the devil," said Abbot Jaloux yesterday. . . . Alas, those unhappy children were never able to recognize the remarkable psychological talents of Abbot Jaloux.

"I despise your odious authority!" That was how they would reply to their masters.

God is just. David Sterne and Michel Rameau died before reaching their twentieth year. May peace be with us, Lord, amen.

Complacency, as we priests know, is an abyss which lies in wait for even the strongest of souls. Remember, Father Antime, God does not like softness. Terror is quelled only with force. One must punish, chastise, humiliate. It is thus that reverence is imposed. (At the sound of my steps, at the sight of my swishing black cassock, they tremble, they are terrified, I hear them muttering, "It is Abbot Jaloux. . . " pathetic little boys who humbly beg you for counsel, confessing tiny faults, how can one resist the temptation to play with their supple consciences, to torture them a little in order to pluck at last like dead fruit the touching repentances which they offer you?)

Hit them without fear, Father Antime, beat their rebellious spines! The whip drives out the dream. We have not punished enough, Michel Rameau and David Sterne were allowed to enjoy themselves too much in our House: a rigorous dawn is at hand!

"How many strokes, Father Abbot, for Leo Cesar who stole an apple from the refectory?"

"Ten strokes."

My brother you have lost everything
Where you are there is
Neither the silence of death   nor sleep
They continue to talk about you how many times will they kill you
I cannot hear your name without shuddering
Don't speak his name   I am betraying him
Charles Sterne   priest   that is all I am
I dare not open my mouth either to defend you
Or to pray   the memory of you overwhelms me
Do not pursue me with your faults have pity
My life is orderly   I hurt no one
But like yourself David   yesterday   I am not happy
They stripped you of everything   they counted
your bones
But if anyone speaks of you   in order to forget you
I shamefully   lower my eyes.

The child which I brought into the world was a good child. But he was stricken with a mysterious illness from which, it seems, he was not meant to recover. David always evaded our care. His brothers liked him, but he seemed to care for no one. From infancy, he had learned to divest himself of all affection. My husband and I thought that he might be happier in the Seminary than at home, since the religious vocation has been a tradition in our family. I recall that David bitterly opposed the idea.

"If you impose upon me a life in which I have had no choice, you will bitterly regret it!" I heard him say to my husband who slapped him on the face in a moment of anger.

"Is that the way to speak to your father?"

I wanted to intervene but I did not dare. There is in our house a great respect for the authority of my husband. And David always refused to behave like the others. . . .

"On your feet! Accused, on your feet!"
                but he did not rise   he smiled at me
insolently   he was vicious that child he was made of
iron there he stood   calmly coolly   blue tie white
shirt he was looking at me slyly   have you thought of
your mother?
    "No."
Why do you steal   since you do not like stealing
    "Bad habit."
                And remorse David Sterne   have you ever
                known it
    "I leave it to you, Your Honor."
Suddenly he was talking of Kant
I listened to him   irritated   fascinated
too bad I thought to let him rot in prison
out of pity I reduced his sentence
I myself have a heart
one gets bored so quickly in this job
Capital punishment is not common these days

as for me   I like action violence
I like to see these young dry-eyed men
walk calmly towards the scaffold
what dignity   what nobility
they scorn the chaplain
who hovers over them with clumsy words
But David Sterne was only a thief
Capricious indifferent rapist thief all the same
He bored me.

I lead them to my place it is my job I protect them
from the police I lull them to sleep   they like kind
words   I ask nothing of them when they have nothing
to give
    "Your place is not at all attractive, old woman, what a
fearful stench, we are going to kill ourselves one of
these days on your rotting staircase!"
they are frank   they lie too   it has been at least
a month since he last came
that wicked little scoundrel   he used to come every day
I can't remember all their names
    "You are old and ugly, your ankles are thick."
He was sixteen maybe, I can't remember all their faces.

Take care, Father Antime, do not shut your eyes for a moment, the devil prowls everywhere. Oh! I have had enough of
those two, Pierre and Samuel Martin! The little vipers, they
sow bad examples everywhere! Ten. . . eleven. . . twelve
strokes of the yardstick on their fingers. But they do not cry.
No, they look straight ahead of them, their lips clenched. This
is the result of their association with Michel Rameau and
David Sterne, an inflexible pride mixed with all the secrets of
lust. But they will fear me one day. . .I have not finished with

79

them yet. Their fingers red, and still they do not cry! I tell you, Father Antime, the errors of the past will not repeat themselves in my presence!

My brother, you have lost everything
Your life has escaped you like a dream
About you there is nothing but weeping and desolation
Do you remember   how as children   we used to
live together
Without ever seeing each other
One of us trembled at the sound of his father's voice
the other smiled
     today I tremble alone
and you rest
I was small and weak   you did not like me
David what did you do   I am so ashamed
We who lived so close to each other in the same house
without ever seeing each other.

One beautiful autumn day, I accompanied Michel and David to a concert. They often came to meet me after school. They used to lend me their books, we sometimes exchanged records. Anyone who saw them for the first time remarked at once as to how they were very charming and polite. My mother liked them.

"Let's go to the woods," Michel said as we emerged from the concert.

We were happy. I recall that David laughed a great deal. He was like a child. But, in the woods, they suddenly stopped. A heavy silence fell over us. It became deeper and deeper. Perhaps it was because it had suddenly become colder, perhaps because the sky had grown dark. I was frightened. Michel and David looked pale.

"I want to go home."

"Come on, little girl," said Michel in a strange voice. We are going to play a terrible game, but you must be sensible. Isn't that right, David?

David laughed. He no longer resembled a child. Suddenly, I did not recognize him. Again, a deep silence fell over us. I cried out, but no one came.

"You must not cry," said David. "Otherwise, I shall have to become brutal."

While I fought off the embrace of Michel, I could feel David's cold hand moving over my breast. I understood then that it was too late. In turn, Michel and David subdued me. I lay there, trembling from the cold and from my nakedness.

Occasionally, their troubled faces pass before me in my dreams. I hear Michel sobbing somewhere nearby, but I cannot see him. Or, if I see him, he quickly disappears.

but you David who then are you
between the shores of death
running   fleeing like a river
the black shores
closing upon you

"What terror for the sinner
  when Our Savior returns
  to preside over His terrible tribunal!"
                    If you had listened to me David your Spiritual

Director your friend you would not be there now
twisted disfigured   by the pitiless flames of hell
Oh! miserable child so consumed with evil   I pitied you
how I pitied you
deliver me Lord
I thirst I thirst   do you recall the cry of the sinner
but all the same they failed to kill me with that ladder
their intention was evil   their hearts inflamed with
hatred
I who loved you so much David   see how I have aged
because of you my shoulders are stooped   my head has
lost all its hair   miserable children who laughed
blasphemed
burn now!

From this day forth, I shall remain silent. I fear my husband
and my children. David, who died alone, remains here between us, separating us. I was a good mother, I prayed for my
son, though I did not visit him in prison. I could not cross the
threshhold of my house without awakening the suspicions of
my husband:
     "I forbid you to see David."
     I could not forget my duties as a wife. It was too late. I
could not resist my husband. And I sensed that David was
already lost. My God, what could I do?

If I had a little courage, I would tell the truth, but I fear my
superiors, Father Antime does not like me, he would be only
too happy to rebuke me, and then I have a wife and four
children, I have no choice but to remain in this vicious Seminary, a livid greenhouse of lies and hypocrisies, I know, I
know, but at fifty years of age how does one embark upon a
new life, I am only a poor teacher of mathematics and Latin,

my wife reminds me often enough of that, but Father Antime, Abbot Jaloux, oh! I know, I know those slow cruel persecutions

David Sterne   Michel Rameau   I know how they
enslaved your souls   broke your brave minds   those
daily punishments those living tortures   (and how many
strokes of the lash were administered behind locked
doors?)
                                                calmly they killed you
I know everything   I understand well this slow descent
toward death
      David   Michel
the most promising of my students   over-endowed with
gifts but I have no authority   I am only a poor teacher
of mathematics. . . .

A certain young man was in the habit of frequenting the same tavern as I. Rather elegant, yes, for a drunkard, but his fingers were stained with nicotine. (He smoked too much.) He had a friend, a strange bird who wore glasses. The two of them used to sit there by the hour, talking. I enjoyed listening to them. I appreciate intelligent conversations.

But one day, these two friends had a quarrel. "Goodbye, Reine, goodbye," said the one, and that was it. I never saw them again. It was purely by chance that I happened to be sitting there. It is always by chance that I take the same seat in the tavern. I drink five or six beers alone, alone like all the others about me, sitting in a pale fog. It is pleasant, especially when one has been selling pencils all day, which is how I make my living. But I was used to seeing those two fellows sitting there alongside me. And now their table is empty. Where are they? People come and go. One should not pay any attention to them. Now, I drink alone, alone each night, and other strangers debate endlessly about me, in the fog. . . .

Oh! little Reine, we have grieved so much for him, he came nearly every day with fresh bread and cheese for the children, he was like God, so gentle, with his big bright eyes, a good little one he was, but what got into his head so suddenly, eh, to go and burn himself alive in the street, that was pure stupidity

we Gobins are little people the rats eat us
                                              it is true
but gratitude   respect   we know
and we still grieve for our little Reine
We are naked and poor like the trees in winter
it is true
But we have hearts   this François Reine had a heart too
He sobbed sobbed like a woman the day Pierre was bitten
by a
                        rat
Everyone meets his fate as for us our fate never changes
that little Reine was burned alive not by fire
                        but by
                              pity.

I do not understand, I do not understand why François Reine

suddenly abandoned me, I was his best friend, his collaborator on the journal *The Idealist's Revolution* and on the Committee of Workers, I do not understand why he suddenly saw the world as a place of terror, of annihilation, delirious with pity, or perhaps with fever, for several months he had seemed somewhat ill, at our final meeting he said to me:

"Gabriel, each day I lose more faith in myself, it seems to me that I am living in a world of assassins, that each one of us is moving each day closer to the end, that nuclear holocaust attends us, and that, moreover, that is what we want, yes, secretly, to kill or be killed. . . ."

These thoughts occupied him to the point that he no longer believed in anything, neither in those social causes which had once inspired him, nor in us, his friends.

"But, François, how can we live without faith? I know that yesterday we were privileged children, but are we not now slowly paying our debt? The misery of the world is immense, and we are too few, that is why we need you. Do not abandon our Committee. We have too much to do, there are right now ten families appealing to us. All those hovels infested with rats, those children dying before they reach the age of five, our work is just beginning. Recover your faith, do not leave us!

I do not understand why he suddenly abandoned
everything
And I think
    of that immense lost tenderness
Whom now will that serve?

François had changed greatly during those final months. It

seemed to me that I no longer knew him. For several weeks, we spoke of ending our relationship. There was always some misunderstanding between us. Yes, it was as if some invisible presence had entered our lives, ceaselessly menacing us. Perhaps he loved another girl? But the most troubling thing was that he no longer attended our conferences, that he had lost all interest in those causes which we had taken up together, that he had become a stranger suddenly to everyone.

"The divine light has left the earth. What is the use?"

"But our love, François? Our ambition to work for the good of humanity?"

There was a dark light in his eyes as he said, "But finally, Brigitte, who are we to believe ourselves called to such a role? Don't you see that there emanates from each one of us, on this Committee, in all that he does, a tyrannical goodness which overwhelms those whom he presumes to aid, permitting not even those who suffer to retain their suffering? If I am here to embrace suffering and poverty, it is no longer enough that I should experience them only for a few hours each day and then return to my comfortable home, no, I must let them permeate every part of my being, possess me. . . ."

I could see him withdrawing from me. I no longer went to see him. A note addressed to an unknown friend was found in his room: these last words confirm that my fiance had lost his reason; otherwise, how could he have died in such confusion?

I have nothing to offer   my agony perhaps
but as you know
it is not very nice to die. . .

FIVE

Silently, his suitcase in hand, François Reine left his room, his cold bed, and taking care not to make a sound, walked in the direction of the station, skirting the sleeping town, which would soon be bathed in the first rays of dawn. But perhaps he lost his way, for an hour later he had still not come in sight of the station. But no, the country through which he passed silently invited him to enter, to stay awhile, a bright country visible from afar (yet very near in the sluggish air), and he imagined the sea, somewhere nearby, long white beaches disappearing into infinity under a bright spring sun. But how could François Reine run freely in the direction of the horizon when the knot of his tie constrained him to the point of suffocation? He ran, all the same, with the calculated elegance of the dreamer, his feet scarcely touching the ground, floating over those hills, those curious dream-like mountains, covering long distances with a single stride. . . .

TRESPASSING IS FORBIDDEN ON THESE BEACHES

MILITARY INSTALLATIONS

DANGER   DANGER

"It is of no importance," thought François, taking off his shoes at the edge of the water. "This beach is public property. . . ."

François Reine did not like signs. It was a matter, therefore, of ignoring them.

TRESPASSERS WILL BE EXECUTED

"Do not listen to them," a voice said to him, "do not listen to anyone. . . ."

François recognized the hazy silhouette of David at the water's edge. He wanted to join him. (Was he not supposed to lend him his Bible?) "I'm coming, I'm coming," he called, but he sensed suddenly that he was being followed, threatened. Turning, he observed a column of soldiers marching toward him, rifles in their hands. . . .

"Do not be frightened," said the lead soldier, "it is not you whom we are after but your friend. Where is he hiding? He robbed a poor woman in the subway. . . ."

"Why all these rifles? One gun would be enough," said François Reine, trembling slightly.

"He must be exterminated, he must be pulled out by the roots!" cried the soldier. "No part of him must be left! Neither body nor soul!"

"But why?" asked François.

"Your friend will not escape us this time," said the soldier. "See how many we are. On earth as it is in heaven." François Reine had a sudden unbearable vision of the skies opening, being torn asunder: at last he understood, the agony of the world had begun. Fiery missiles ploughed the pale blue sky. In their wake was sown death and destruction.

"What are you doing here at this hour?" asked the soldier. "Shouldn't you be at the University? Faculty of bombs is on your right, just a little farther, quick march!" he shouted, pushing François Reine in the rear. "Obey orders!"

FORBIDDEN   FORBIDDEN

"Do not listen to them," pleaded David, "do not listen to them!"

In the distance, François heard rifle-fire. Several moments later, he stumbled upon the corpse of David on the beach.

"Forbidden to look at him," said the soldier, "to your right, quick march, obey order or you too will be killed!"

Standing before his comrades, François Reine was reading the paper which he had written *On The Inner Development Of Courage,* but no one was listening to him. He was being laughed at in the class.

"When so many others die, it is a scandal. . . ."

> You amuse us Reine
> Poor little man
> You truly amuse us

sang the students in chorus

> oh! he is funny
> he is so funny. . .
> He appeals to those of us

who have consciences
but of course we have consciences
like a dead fish
in an empty acquarium

To the laboratory! To the laboratory!

Indignant at this collective fury, François found himself in the room of Course B607/2.

beat him whip him
poor Reine
he wants so much to be useful

"You have much to learn," said the young soldier, striking François in the face (then spitting against the wall), the divine technique is ours, amen!

In the factories I saw how they manufactured
crime   death
they called it the Aurora
the scientific dawn of happiness
I saw thousands of young men
who had come there to invent new murders

"Isn't that the famous faculty of bombs?"
   "What would become of art without victims? Follow me to the cellar. . . ."

An anemic multitude was enclosed therein
Men women children
Suffering in silence

"No, you are mistaken, François Reine. These are not men.
We have a deep respect for the human race. Rats, I tell you,
they are nothing but rats. . . ."
    His crude laughter filled the room.

They looked at me out of their waxen eyes
    "Rats, and we shall exterminate every one of them!"

Funny François Reine
but all the same confess
that there are too many of this grey race
green race they grow like mushrooms
we have found the solution
a cellar for the rats

It is true that these men who had long been accustomed to
living so far beneath the surface of the earth, in the heavy
humidity of the sewers, still possessed the capacity to grow
smaller, to shrink to the perfect dimensions of rats. . . .
    "Then," said the soldier, "we shall be able to complete our
task without remorse."

Two hundred and fifty thousand children killed since. . .
no serious care given to the wounded. . . no concern. . .

The evening newspaper lay on the table. François Reine was so tired of being cold. Seeking a little warmth, he rapped on David's door, but there was no reply.

"I have come to say goodbye to you
but in vain,
it was too late."

(François, you have not been home for so long,
your father and I are worried about you, write
to me, to the mother who loves you. . .)

François Reine still had several letters to write before leaving for mass. ("Dear Mother, everything is fine, the exams are approaching, as you know, perhaps I shall come home on Sunday, but do not expect me. . . .")

I Have nothing to offer David   nothing
my agony perhaps
But as you know   it is not very nice to. . . .

François Reine dropped his head into his hands. He laughed quietly, for his decision had finally been taken, and in spite of everything, he thought, he was still happy. . . .

DATE DUE
DATE DE RETOUR
